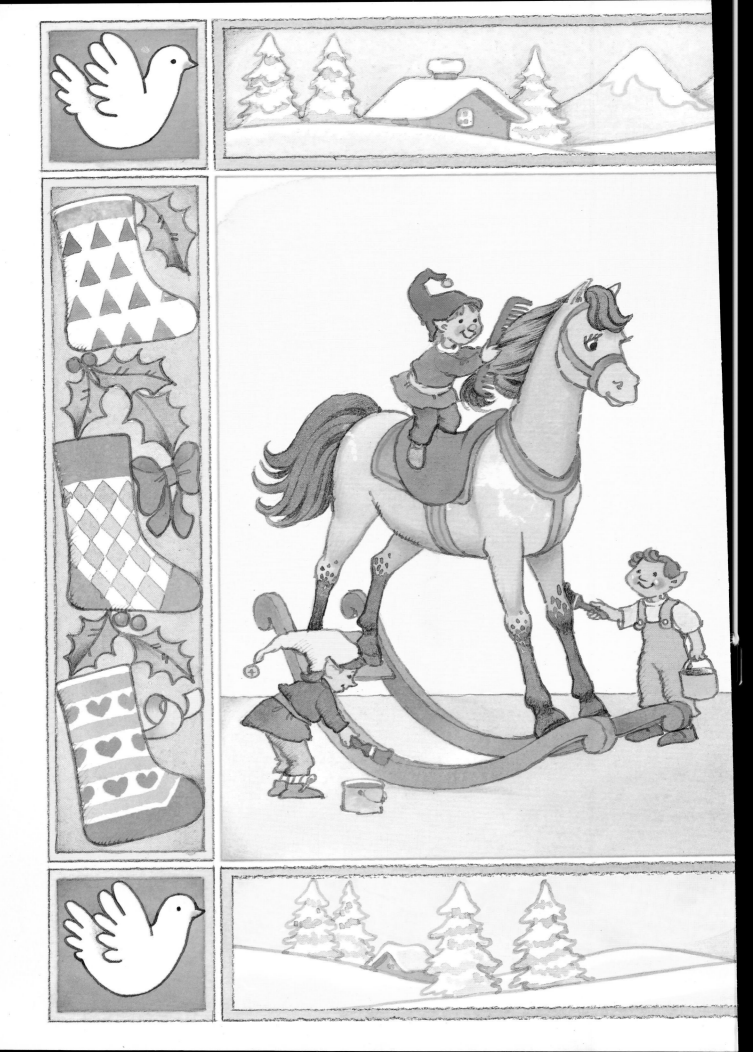

He sprang to his sleigh,
     to his team gave a whistle,
And away they all flew
     like the down of a thistle.
But I heard him exclaim,
     as he drove out of sight,
"Merry Christmas to all,
     and to all a good night!"

Soon gave me to know I had nothing to dread.
    He spoke not a word, but went straight to his work,
And filled all the stockings; then turned with a jerk,
    And laying his finger aside of his nose,
And giving a nod, up the chimney he rose;

He had a broad face and a little round belly,
    That shook when he laughed, like a bowl full of jelly.
He was chubby and plump - a right jolly old elf -
    And I laughed when I saw him, in spite of myself.
A wink of his eye and a twist of his head,

His eyes - how they twinkled! His dimples how merry!
  His cheeks were like roses, his nose like a cherry!
His droll little mouth was drawn up like a bow,
  And the beard on his chin was as white as the snow;
The stump of a pipe he held tight in his teeth,
  And the smoke it encircled his head like a wreath:

As I drew in my head, and was turning around,
  Down the chimney St. Nicholas came with a bound.
He was dressed all in fur, from his head to his foot,
  And his clothes were all tarnished with ashes and soot;
A bundle of toys he had flung on his back,
  And he looked like a peddler just opening his pack.

To the top of the porch! to the top of the wall!
  Now dash away! dash away! dash away all!"
As dry leaves that before the wild hurricane fly,
  When they meet with an obstacle, mount to the sky,
So up to the house-top the coursers they flew,
  With the sleigh full of toys, and St. Nicholas too.
And then in a twinkle, I heard on the roof,
  The prancing and pawing, of each little hoof.

More rapid than eagles his coursers they came,
    And he whistled, and shouted, and called them by name:
"Now, Dasher! now, Dancer! now, Prancer and Vixen!
    On, Comet! on, Cupid! on, Donner and Blitzen!

Away to the window I flew like a flash,
    Tore open the shutters, and threw up the sash.
The moon on the breast of the new-fallen snow,
    Gave the lustre of midday to objects below;
When, what to my wondering eyes should appear,
    But a miniature sleigh and eight tiny reindeer,
With a little old driver, so lively and quick,
    I knew in a moment, it must be St. Nick.

Mama in her kerchief, and I in my cap,
  Had just settled down for a long winter's nap;
When out on the lawn there arose such a clatter,
  I sprang from my bed to see what was the matter.

The children were nestled
all snug in their beds,
While visions of sugar-plums
danced in their heads;

The stockings were hung
by the chimney with care,
In hopes that St. Nicholas
soon would be there;

'Twas the night before Christmas,
   when all through the house
Not a creature was stirring,
   not even a mouse;

THE NIGHT BEFORE CHRISTMAS

Illustrated by Ken McKie.